In these reflective pieces, Irene Zimmerman has recrafted the biblical message in ways that touch the imagination. With remarkable perception, she has grasped the spirit of the passage, creatively reinterpreting it. At times she rereads the script of the text, releasing its dynamism and challenging the reader with its radical simplicity. At other times she embellishes the story after the manner of Jewish midrash, filling in its gaps with contemporary concerns and insights. The strength of her imagery is both in its artistic refinement and in its unabashed humanism. With her pen she has brought the Bible to life anew. **Dianne Bergant, CSA,** Catholic Theological Union, Chicago

Irene Zimmerman is a poet, and does what poets do. She overrides categories, breaks conventions, says it new, and moves us to where we gasp in the presence of gift. Some say imagination is linked to the Holy Spirit. So it is here, spirit of freedom, spirit of healing, spirit of joy. Un-bent, all tall and unencumbered. I find the words come off the page to our own unbending. Irene says Mary's word is "yes." Here it is God's "yes" to any listener. I am glad I am among them. **Walter Brueggemann,** Columbia Theological Seminary, Decatur, Georgia

This poetry mediates an original insight into the mysteries of the life of Christ, and the simple beauty of the language makes them not only illuminating but touching. **Sandra M. Schneiders, IHM,** Jesuit School of Theology at Berkeley, Berkeley, California

Poetry has many tasks: refinement of the heart, enhancement of life, restoring hope and joy. In *Woman Un-Bent* we experience those tasks accomplished and are drawn more deeply into Gospel living. **Robert F. Morneau,** auxiliary bishop of Green Bay, Wisconsin

To put it in Irish, there's a power of storytelling in this engaging collection of poems. There is a freshness, a spark. The author, with insight guiding imagination, looks closely at what is said and what is left unsaid in a span of Gospel accounts. Throughout the book, Zimmerman highlights women coming into their own among those healed, in the circle of disciples, and in carrying the Good News. **James Torrens, SJ,** *America*

When responding to and interpreting the Scriptures, Zimmerman brings to her poems and stories the authority of a Christian imagination. **Eleanor Fitzgibbons, IHM,** poet in residence, Marygrove College, Detroit

The stories in the Scriptures are about God, the Word made flesh, and ordinary people called to a mysterious role in the history of salvation. To tell those stories, the Scriptures needed classical images, symbols, and poetic language. To retell and interpret those stories, we also need the same. We can thank Irene Zimmerman for dedicating her poetic gift to the stories of the Scriptures. With her we not only understand the word of God, we contemplate it. **Eugene LaVerdiere, SSS,** *Emmanuel*

Irene Zimmerman's *Woman Un-Bent* is a thought-provoking, deeply insightful look into the minds and hearts of the people whose lives are revealed in the Scriptures. In midrashic style her poems explore the thoughts and feelings of these ancient people who were forever transformed through a profound encounter with God. Readers can see their own life mirrored in the actions and responses of these original witnesses. **Shannon Schrein, OSF,** Lourdes College, Sylvania, Ohio

# Woman Un-Bent

Irene Zimmerman, OSF

Saint Mary's Press
Christian Brothers Publications
Winona, Minnesota

The publishing team included Michael Wilt, development editor; Laurie A. Berg, copy editor; James H. Gurley, production editor; Hollace Storkel, typesetter; Maurine R. Twait, art director; pre-press, printing, and binding by the graphics division of Saint Mary's Press.

Cover painting: *Christ in the House of Martha and Mary,* by Johannes Vermeer, National Gallery of Scotland. Used with permission.

The acknowledgments continue on page 110.

Printed in the United States of America ·

Printing: 9 8 7 6 5 4 3 2

Year: 2007 06 05 04 03 02 01 00

ISBN 0-88489-585-8

Genuine recycled paper with 10 % post-consumer waste.
Printed with soy-based ink.

To two School Sisters of Saint Francis:

Sr. Lorraine Aspenleiter,
spiritual director,
who through her wisdom, strength, and simplicity
has led me to experience God as Mentor and Friend;

Sr. Theophane Hytrek,
internationally recognized composer and organist,
whose compositions of liturgical music
continue to lead me to experience God as Beauty
and whose encouragement during life and urging from
heaven
impelled me to write this book.

# Contents

# Preface

The initial inspiration for most of the poems and stories in this book came during periods of reflection. At the time of my first directed retreat, my director gave me clear and simple directions on how to meditate on the Scriptures. "Ask the Holy Spirit to help you," she said. "Read the passage. Read it several times. Use your imagination to see, hear, touch, smell, and taste what's there. Then let the Holy Spirit talk to you about it." As I walked the woods and fields, contemplating wild lilies, listening to birds, picking and eating fruit from trees, I did, indeed, begin to see, hear, touch, smell, and taste the Scriptures. And I renewed my appreciation of imagination as a gift meant to help us pray

In the twenty years since that first directed retreat, the four Gospels have been my primary *lectio divina*. Usually my reading includes the footnotes; occasionally it expands to the related Scripture passages noted there. With each rereading—sometimes covering a passage in an hour, sometimes staying with a passage for several weeks—I come to fresh insights.

Reading the Gospels sequentially in this way has led me to discover and probe many stories of women to whom Jesus brought the Good News. This has become good news for me as I see how Jesus—disregarding the cultic mores of his society—conversed with women in public places, healed them, defended them, befriended them, and called them to discipleship. Yet their stories appear only rarely in the lectionary and even less frequently in the Sunday homily. These women, marginalized in the Jewish society because of their gender, remain on the fringes of Christian consciousness today. Some of their stories are told in this book.

In the Gospels of Mark and Matthew, the messenger at the empty tomb charges the women to tell the other disciples that Jesus is risen and is going ahead of them to Galilee, where they will see him. The disciples are invited to go back to the beginning of their encounter with the One who is now risen. There, as they once again follow him through Galilean towns and countryside and to the provinces beyond, they will finally recognize the One who walks ahead of them.

And so will we! Surely this good news is not intended only for the disciples who knew Jesus in his human lifetime and for the early Christians to whom the Evangelists addressed the Gospels. All who follow Jesus are urged to return to the beginning and start over.

But if we really follow closely behind this Jesus, we need to be forewarned. We see him ministering to the marginalized of *his* day, encountering hometown "realists" who have no faith, and challenging the hardhearted hypocrites who eventually crucify him. At some point we will be compelled either to leave him altogether or to do the work he calls us to do in *our* day. And this could mean crucifixion. The good news, of course, is that Christ walks ahead of us through death into life.

With these poems and stories, I invite you to walk into the Gospels where "he is going ahead of you to Galilee; there you will see him" (Matthew 28:7; Mark 16:7).

Irene Zimmerman
Alverno College
Advent 1998

# I

# Incarnation

Then Mary's word: *Yes!*
rose like a pillar of fire,
and Breath blew creation
into Christed crystal.

*(Incarnation)*

# First Forgiveness

The usually mild evening breeze
became a wailing wind
as the gates clanged shut behind them.

They shivered despite their leathery clothes
as they searched for the fragrant blossoms
they'd grown accustomed to sleep on,
but found only serpentine coils
that bit and drew blood from their hands.

It was Eve who discovered the cave.
When she emerged, she saw Adam
standing uncertainly at the entrance.

A river of fire flooded her face
as she remembered his blaming words—
"The woman you gave me,
she gave me fruit from the tree,
and I ate."

"Spend the night wherever you choose,"
she told him bitterly.
"You needn't stay with me."

Long afterward, when even the moon's
cold light had left the entrance
and she'd made up a word
for the hot rain running from her eyes,
she sensed Adam near her in the dark.

His breath shivered on her face.
"Eve," he moaned,
"I'm sorry. Forgive me."

In the darkness between them,
the unfamiliar words
waited, quivering.
She understood their meaning
when she touched his tears.

# First Parenting

In early years, while Adam tilled the fields
and Eve filled her lap with baby boys and girls,
they watched attentively for signs of aberration,
pounced hard on spats between the two- and three-
year-olds, planted frequent kisses on each child's
cheek, and tried to model love between them.

Later, as their growing sons and daughters
left the house, arm in arm, to play their made-up games,
they followed them with anxious admonitions—
"Don't fight! Take care of one another!"—knowing
they had brought a blight into their children's souls.

In the years of grieving for their twin sons—
the one whose blood had reddened the yellow grain
of sacrifice, the other branded for all time
as murderer—they asked each other,
"What could God have been thinking of
to give us power to choose to love or hate?"

Gradually, as Adam's handsome curls turned white
and Eve's beloved face shriveled like an apple,
they saw that God had led them back, if not
to Paradise itself, to love at least—
the best of what that early world had offered.

"Will our children live in peace after we're gone?"
they wondered in the end as they came to know
the pain of powerlessness and something of
an unfathomable God who dared to take
the risk of losing them, for their own freedom's sake.

# Sarah's Laughter

(Genesis 18:1–15)

When Abraham had hurried back
to the three Strangers with bread
and meat, milk and curds,
Sarah, obediently hiding her faded
beauty behind the tent flaps,
watched them feasting beneath the oak.

From there the Strangers' words
came winging to where she stood—
in shocked disbelief at first,
having grown old and used to
the sterile disfavor of Abraham's God,
then exploding in peals of laughter
that ricocheted off the oaks of Mamre
and the stony hills of promise.

"How many can you count, Sarah?"
Abraham asked as they held each other
beneath a blanket of stars.
"How many children will there be?"
The words set her off again,
and Abraham too,
with irrepressible mirth
till the hills whooped and hollered
and the stars blazed their *Aha*
in the pregnant desert night.

# "How Can This Be, Since I Am a Virgin?"
(Luke 1:34)

Your world hung in the balance of her *yes* or *no*.
Yet, "She must feel absolutely free," You said,
and chose with gentle sensitivity not to go
Yourself—to send a messenger instead.

I like to think You listened in at that interview
with smiling admiration and surprise
to that humble child who—
though she didn't amount to much in Jewish eyes,
being merely virgin, not yet come to bloom—
in the presence of that otherworldly Power
crowding down the walls and ceiling of her room,
did not faint or cry or cower
and could not be coerced to enflesh Your covenant,
but asked her valid question first
before she gave her full and free consent.

I like to think You stood
to long applaud such womanhood.

# Incarnation

In careful hands
God held the molten world—
fragile filigree
of unfinished blown glass.

Then Mary's word: *Yes!*
rose like a pillar of fire,
and Breath blew creation
into Christed crystal.

# Women Weaving

(Luke 1:39–55)

Afterward, Mary moved from fear
(*Will they drag me to the stoning place?*)
to pain (*Will Joseph doubt my faithfulness?*)
to trust (*I fear no evil—Thou art with me.*)
and back again to fear. "I must go to my cousin,"
she said, and set out in haste for Judea.

As her feet unraveled the warp and woof
of valleys and hills, darkness and days
from Nazareth to Elizabeth,
Mary busily wove the heart of her Son.

When her newly-womaned cousin came,
Elizabeth, wise old weaver herself
for several months by then, instantly
saw the signs and heavily ran to meet her.

"Who am I," she called, "that the mother
of my Lord should come to visit me?"
and helplessly held her sides as laughter
shuttled back and forth inside her.

Then Mary sang the seamless song
she'd woven on the way.

# Unto His Own

(Luke 2:5–20)

Homeless that first night—
one more statistic
to add to the census,
one more mouth to feed.

Only the shepherds,
having nothing to lose
except a little sleep,
came to see.

# First Word

Mary stirred a measure of flour
into the leaven and listened to Jesus
giggle and coo through the sounds of languages
living and dead. She laughed as she added
a second cup to the bubbling batter—
for all she knew, her son could be babbling
in Greek.

She added a third measure, worked it
into the glutinous mass, and added
a fourth. As she scraped the sides of the bowl,
she remembered the scrape of the olive tree
against her father's house while she listened,
inside, to words more foreign than any
her son was speaking now.

She was up to her wrists in the sticky dough
when Jesus arrived at the initial sounds
of his native tongue. She flew from kitchen
to carpenter shop, floured her husband's
hand midway between awl and hammer,
and ran back with him.

Their cradled son, his fingers and toes
curling around the olive-wood rattle
that Joseph had lately carved for him,
was distinctly repeating the Aleph and Beth
of his native tongue to the leavening dough
and spellbound table and chairs:
*"Abba, Abba, Abba."*

# Litany for Ordinary Time

Mary, queen of the ordinary—
    queen of spinning wheel and loom
        who wove from ordinary stuff
        the flawless fabric of
        God's humanness;

    queen whose pregnancy
        put Joseph's other plans aside
        and sent his saw singing
        into cradlewood;

    queen of water jars daily filled,
        of swaddling clothes spread outdoors
        to dry, of scrubbed floors
        and everlastingly sawdusty son;

    queen of skinned knees,
        splintered fingers,
        aching stomach, fevered head,
        herbal teas;

    queen of fresh-baked bread
        whose wheaty power
        put flesh on growing boy
        and joy at evening meal—

Mary, queen of ordinary time and space,
thank you for your ordinary grace.

**II**

# The Testing

Who would walk with them
in the winter seasons
and in that sunless valley
where there are no reasons?
*(From the Pinnacle)*

# The Testing

(Luke 4:1–13)

> *who, though he was in the form of God,*
> *did not regard equality with God*
> *as something to be exploited,*
> *but emptied himself.*
>> *(Philippians 2:6–7)*

## 1. Loaves of Stone

Watching the slant light of morning
finger the stones of the wall he had built
to shelter himself from cold night winds,
he sensed that before the sun had burned out

on the other end of the wilderness,
the trials would show their evil faces.
Filled with dread, he got up from his mat
and knelt to beg for strength to endure.

Words at last washed over him:
"Have no fear. I am with you.
I myself will tell you what to say!"
He arose, refreshed, ready.

Hunger seized him—an alien creature
gnawing his insides, engorging itself,
snaking up from the pit of his stomach
into his chest, his throat, his mouth.

At arm's reach, the top row of stones
glowed smooth and round as the loaves
his mother had baked and set on the shelf
to cool when he was a growing boy.

A thought padded into his mind,
mewed around and around his senses.
"If you are the Son of God," it purred,
"try out your 'Abba, cadabra.'"

"If you asked the Father for bread,
would he give you a stone?"
Its tongue searched the hollows
of his hunger, exquisitely licking, licking.

Bewildered, Jesus looked at the stones.
On the morning of the world,
they had tumbled forth from God's mouth
to be building blocks, not bread.

They had sheltered him
and would shelter others after him—
unless, to placate his hunger,
he made them pawns of his power.

He would not do it.
"One does not live by bread alone,"
he said with finality, "but by every word
that comes from the mouth of God."

Hunger snarled, but slithered away.

## 2. The Reign of God

Higher, still higher they climbed,
till all the kingdoms of the world
shone below them in the sun—
the vast lands,
the jeweled seas.

"All these kingdoms are mine," Jesus heard,
"to give to whomever I please.
To you then I give their glory
and all this authority
if you will worship me."

Jesus turned and saw the world
scintillating in those eyes.
"All yours," he heard again,
the royal words offered to him
like a jeweled crown.

He looked back to where the lands and seas
still lay in calm, expansive splendor,
open to sun, bonded to sky.
"Brothers! Sisters!" he called to them,
his arms stretching wide as a cross.

And to that usurper, as he crept away,
Jesus commanded, "It is written,
'Worship the Lord your God alone.'"

## 3. From the Pinnacle

From that height he saw rivers of pilgrims
streaming down Judean hills, surging up
the Cedron valley, pouring through
the city gates, swirling toward the Temple.
The sacred stairs below him jammed
with flotsam and jetsam.
A sweet-sour stench steamed up
of burning feathers, wool, incense.

A hot breath whispered: "The people
have gathered to renew the Covenant
with the One who promised a Messiah.

If you are the Son of God,
throw yourself down that they may know it.
For it is written, 'He will command his angels
concerning you,' and 'They will bear you up
so that you will not dash your foot against a stone.'"

Jesus imagined himself leaping from the ledge
of his humanness—Yahweh's darling
defying the laws of ordinary flesh,
plummeting down toward the terrified crowd,
then caught and enthroned on seraphic wings.
From there he swung like a golden censer
pouring down blessings on pilgrims who came,
year after year, to adore him.

Was this the leap of faith the Spirit was urging?

Through a blur of incense, he began to recognize
faces of friends and neighbors whose tables
and chairs he had made and mended.
When they returned to their fields and flocks,
their planting and harvesting, washing and baking,
lovemaking and childbearing,
what good would it do them to know
the Messiah awaited their yearly worship?

Who would walk with them
in the winter seasons
and in that sunless valley
where there are no reasons?

"Leave me," he thundered. "Again it is written,
'Do not put the Lord your God to the test.'"

Even as the evil one slunk from his sight,
Jesus knew he would meet it again.

# III
# Mission and Discipleship

She stood up straight and let
God's glory touch her face.

*(Woman Un-Bent)*

# Cana Wine

(John 2:1–11)

"The weather's so hot
and no more wine's to be bought
in all of Cana!
It's just what I feared—
just why I begged my husband
to keep the wedding small."

"Does he know?" Mary asked.

"Not yet. Oh, the shame!
Look at my son and his beautiful bride!
They'll never be able
to raise their heads again,
not in this small town."

"Then don't tell him yet."

Mary greeted the guests
as she made her way
through crowded reception rooms.
"I must talk to you, Son,"
she said unobtrusively.

Moments later he moved
toward the back serving rooms.
They hadn't seen each other
since the morning he'd left her—
before the baptism
and the desert time.

There was so much to tell her,
so much to ask.
But this was not the time!

They could talk tomorrow
on the way to Capernaum.

She spoke urgently, her words
both request and command to him:
"They have no wine."

But he hadn't been called yet!
He hadn't felt it yet.
Would she send him so soon
to the hounds and jackals?
For wine?

Was wine so important then?

"Woman, what concern is that
to you and me?
My hour has not yet come."

Her unflinching eyes reflected to him
his twelve-year-old self
telling her with no contrition:
"Why were you searching for me?
Did you not know that I must be
in my Father's house?"

She left him standing there—
vine from her stock,
ready for fruit bearing—
and went to the servants.
"Do whatever he tells you," she said.

From across the room
she watched them fill water jars,
watched the chief steward
drink from the dripping cup,
saw his eyes open in wide surprise.

She watched her grown son
toast the young couple,
watched the groom's parents
and the guests raise their cups.

She saw it all clearly:
saw the Best Wine
pouring out for them all.

# Homecoming

(Mark 6:1–4)

Unclean spirits
stormed from their victims,
loudly shrieking
their furious witness:
"What do you want of us,
Holy One of God?"

A tiger sea,
its foaming jaws ready
to tear boat and fishermen
caught in its claws,
turned kitten-tame
and lay at his feet.

But Nazarene neighbors
faithfully stuck to
their wide reputation
of narrow meanness
and ran their carpenter-son
out of town.

# Cure of the Paralytic

(Mark 2:1–12)

There were some who insisted
that Jacob's paralysis
was punishment for his secret sins
and he wasn't worth our pity.
But when we heard about the leper
who showed up cured by Jesus,
we four got together.
"There ought to be a way," we said,
"to help Jacob too."

When we got to Jesus' place,
the crowd wouldn't let us through,
what with the mat and all.
"Why not try the roof?"
someone said, laughing.
We looked at one another.
We'd come too far for nothing.
"Let's try it!" we said.

We edged around the crowd
to the back of the house,
hoisted up mat and Jacob,
and poked a hole in the thatch.
The oily voices of Jerusalem scribes,
heckling Jesus, seeped up to us.
"Let's give the Master a break," we said,
and tore the roof apart.

We lowered the litter
and swung ourselves down
in a rain of dust and straw.

The scribes sputtered and coughed
into gold-embroidered sleeves
and retreated to the corners.
But Jesus smiled us a welcome,
brushed the straw from his shoulders,
and turned his eyes toward Jacob.

The room watched in silence
as the Master leaned down to touch him.
"Your sins are forgiven," he said.
As rumbling rose from the shadows,
Jesus' command rang clear:
"Stand up! Take your bed and go home!"

Jacob sprang up like a wheat stalk
and carried his mat out the door.

We stayed to listen to Jesus
as he shone in a shaft of light,
the dust we had raised
forming an aura around him.

# Blind Trust

(Mark 10:46–52)

Bartimaeus sat outside
the town of Jericho.
The more they told him where to go,
the louder he cried.

He had no pride—
when Jesus asked, he simply stated:
"Lord, I want to see!" and waited
to be eyed.

# Encounter
# with the Canaanite Woman

(Matthew 15:21–28)

The Canaanite woman, interrupting the company's
retreat by the sea, shouted in deep distress,
"Have mercy on me, Lord, Son of David;
my daughter is tormented by a demon."
But he did not answer her at all.

When the disciples (faithful sons of the house
of Israel, who had left everything to follow him)
urged him to "Send her away, for she keeps
shouting after us," he told her, "I was sent
only to the lost sheep of the house of Israel."

What was the tone of his words? the intent?
Were they meant to thunder her into silence?
Was he following dictates definitively taught
by the scribes (Thou shalt not talk to Gentiles.
Thou shalt not talk in public to women.)?

Was it his tiredness, the heat, the light searing
off the sand, the awareness that what she was asking
was no mere miracle, but a vast hurricane of events
that would send the house of Israel reeling off the rock
where it had stood for a millennium and more

which prompted him to answer her plea with
"It is not fair to take the children's food and throw it
to the dogs"—words congruent with the tradition
that had caused the Israelite fathers to cleanse the tribe
by sending their pagan wives whining back to Canaan?

Or was he trying to probe the depth of the mother lode—
the faith of a mother who, faced with her daughter's dying,
had sent her own fearsome demons flying?
She knelt at his feet—this woman from the coast—
as her wise brothers from the East had done long ago

when they finally found him in his mother's arms,
blissfully content and unaware of their homage.
Did her womb-love plumb the unfathomable well
of his own compassion? (Hath not a Gentile eyes, hands,
organs, dimensions, senses, affections, passions?)

Could it be that she, by the faith and force
of her wit—"Yes, Lord, yet even the dogs
eat the crumbs that fall from their masters' table"—
crumbled the unpalatable crusts of the fathers
and showed him it was right and just

to pull the tablecloth down, spread it out
on the sand (How endlessly it stretched—
a white field to harvest!)
for Jews and Gentiles, sons and daughters
to sit and feast together beside healing waters?

# At Jacob's Well

(John 4)

## 1. Exchange

"Please," he repeated, "I'm thirsty.
Give me a drink." The words
hung in the air between them
like a hand extended in peace.

Shocked, distrustful, she seized
her only weapon. "You people,"
she spat, "think we're nothing but scum.
Here's a cupful of scum if you want it."

He drank her bitter face.
"If you knew the gift of God," he began,
probing her arid soul
with careful divining rod.

They sat and talked for a spell.
She gave him a cup of water.
He gave her a well.

## 2. Reconciliation

He watched as she came up
the path to the well. The apple
of noonday sun hung heavy
and ripe on Mount Gerezim.

He had watched Abraham,
with Sarah, swear the Covenant
and build his altar
on the mountain's heights

and had watched their children's children,
still trumpeting Jericho's fall,
return to renew the Covenant
at the altar of the mountain.

He had watched and waited
for generations and generations
as the tribes wandered again.
He was tired and thirsty from waiting.

"Woman, give me a drink,"
he begged, shattering to shards
the laws dividing Jew from Samaritan,
men from women, clean from unclean.

"How can you, a Jew, ask a woman
of Samaria for a drink?" she scolded,
parrying his peacemaking
with her empty cup.

"Woman, broken by broken covenants,"
he said, "leave these man-made
laws and buckets. Take the truth
of Living Water, springing up inside you,

and carry it to your people
Tell them the prophet they wait for—
the I AM who told you everything—
is waiting for them at the well."

After her telling, all Samaria
came out to drink his words.
The black sheep of Israel
grew fat again on the flowing hills.

Joseph rested at last in peace
at the well of his father, Jacob.
And in her burial cave in Hebron,
Sarah's brittle bones dissolved in laughter.

## 3. To Jesus at the Well

Midnight dew,
grown now to
dayspring, waiting in
parched noon for woman
to bring her heavy jars
to draw water from a tired well,

teach her
to seek wells
beyond her dreaming—
to leave battered buckets at
dead cisterns and clean the debris
from the living spring inside her.

Christ, guide her to that flowing sea.

# Firstborn Sons
# and the Widow of Nain
(Luke 7:11–15)

Jesus halted on the road outside Nain
where a woman's wailing drenched the air.
Out of the gates poured a somber procession
of dark-shawled women, hushed children,
young men bearing a litter that held
a body swathed in burial clothes,
and the woman, walking alone.

> *A widow then—another bundle*
> *of begging rags at the city gates.*
> *A bruised reed!*

Her loud grief labored and churned in him till
"Halt!" he shouted.

The crowd, the woman, the dead man stopped.
Dust, raised by sandaled feet,
settled down again on the sandy road.
Insects waited in shocked silence.

He walked to the litter, grasped a dead hand.
"Young man," he called
in a voice that shook the walls of Sheol,
"I command you, rise!"

The linens stirred.
Two firstborn sons from Nazareth and Nain
met, eye-to-eye.

He placed the pulsing hand into hers.
"Woman, behold your son," he smiled.

# Bethany Decisions

(Luke 10:38–42)

As Jesus taught the gathered brothers
and Martha boiled and baked their dinner,
Mary eavesdropped in the anteroom
between the great hall and the kitchen.
Her dying mother's warning words
clanged clearly in her memory—
"Obey your sister. She has learned
the ways and duties of a woman."

She'd learned her sister's lessons well
and knew a woman's place was *not*
to sit and listen and be taught.
But when she heard the voice of Jesus
call to her above the din
of Martha's boiling pots and pans,
she made her choice decisively—
took off her apron and traditions,
and walked in.

# Jesus and Zacchaeus:
# A Short Story

(Luke 19:1–10)

Too short to see,
Zacchaeus climbed a tree.

Most folks wouldn't give tuppence
for such comeuppance,

but when Jesus saw him
far out on a limb,

he called to that sinner,
"Come down and make dinner."

Zacchaeus gave away
all his ill-gotten pay.
He grew tall that day.

# Woman Un-Bent

(Luke 13:10–17)

That Sabbath day as always
she went to the synagogue
and took the place assigned her
right behind the grill where,
the elders had concurred,
she would block no one's view,
she could lean her heavy head,
and (though this was not said)
she'd give a good example to
the ones who stood behind her.

That day, intent as always
on the Word (for eighteen years
she'd listened thus), she heard
Authority when Jesus spoke.

Though long stripped
of forwardness,
she came forward, nonetheless,
when Jesus summoned her.

"Woman, you are free
of your infirmity," he said.

The leader of the synagogue
worked himself into a sweat
as he tried to bend the Sabbath
and the woman back in place.

But she stood up straight and let
God's glory touch her face.

**IV**

# Dying . . .

the crossbeamed Christ
pours himself out
till rivers run red with
wine enough to satisfy
century-cries of thirst.

*(Crucifixion)*

# Woman Taken in Adultery

(John 8:2–11)

From the angry crunch of their sandaled feet
as they left the courtyard, Jesus knew,
without looking up from his writing on the ground,
that the Pharisees and scribes still carried their stones.

The woman stood where they'd shoved her,
her hair hanging loose over neck and face,
her hands still shielding her head
from the stones she awaited.

"Woman," he asked, "has no one condemned you?"

The heap of woman shuddered, unfolded.
She viewed the courtyard—empty now—
with wild, glazed eyes, and turned back to him.
"No one, Sir," she said, unsurely.

Compassion flooded him like a wadi after rain.
He thought of his mother—had she known such fear?—
and of the gentle man whom he had called *Abba*.
Only when Joseph lay dying had he confided
his secret anguish on seeing his betrothed
swelling up with seed not his own.

"Neither do I condemn you," Jesus said.
"Go your way and sin no more."

Black eyes looked out from an ashen face,
empty, uncomprehending.
Then life rushed back.
She stood before him like a blossoming tree.

"Go in peace and sin no more,"
Jesus called again as she left the courtyard.

He had bought her at a price, he knew.
The stony hearts of her judges
would soon hurl their hatred at him.
His own death was a mere stone's throw away.

# Anointings in Bethany
(John 12:1–8)

Solemnly, Mary entered the room,
holding high the alabaster jar.
It gleamed in the lamplight as she circled the room,
incensing the disciples, blessing Martha's banquet.
"A splendid table!" Mary called with her eyes
as she whirled past her sister.

She came to a halt at last before Jesus,
bowed profoundly and knelt at his feet.
Deftly, she filled her right hand with nard,
placed the jar on the floor,
took one foot in her hands
and moved fragrant fingers across his instep.

Over and over she made the journey
from heel to toes, thanking him
for every step he had made
on Judea's stony hills,
for every stop at their home,
for bringing back Lazarus.

She poured out more nard,
took his other foot in her hands
and started again with strong, rhythmic strokes.
She felt her hands' heat draw out his tiredness,
take away the rebuffs he had known—
the shut doors, the shut hearts.

Energy flowed like a river between them.

· His saturated skin gleamed with oil.

She had no towel!

In an instant she pulled off her veil,
pulled the pins from her hair,
shook it out till it fell in cascades,
and once more cradled each foot,
dried the ankles, the insteps,
drew the strands between his toes.

Without warning, Judas Iscariot
spat out his anger, the words hissing
like lightning above her unveiled head:
"Why was this perfume not sold
for three hundred denarii
and the money given to the poor?"

"Leave her alone!"
Jesus silenced the usurper.
"She bought it so that she might keep it
for the day of my burial."

The words poured like oil,
anointing her from head to foot.

# Entry

(Matthew 21:1–11)

The stage is set
and everything washed clean
in a rain of sunshine.

Hands reach out
to calm a skittish colt,
bewildered by its burden.

The Son of David
rides a rainbowed road
that rocks with hosannas.

# Liberation

(Luke 21:37–38)

*He has brought down the powerful from their thrones,*
*and lifted up the lowly.*

*(Luke 1:52)*

After he had released the doves
and overturned the tables and chairs
of the moneychangers, Jesus spent
the days before his final Passover
proclaiming Good News to humble folk
from as far away as Galilee.

These sat exalted on the sacred steps,
listening to their Beloved Son
stump Herodians, Sadducees,
Pharisees, scribes,
while doves hovered over him
with bright, bright wings.

# Legacy

When he was a child
his mother told him
of how she and Joseph
had been turned away
from their ancestral home—
the House of Bread—
on the night of his birth.

The story taught him
that rejection and hunger
gnawed with the same teeth.

Grown, he walked through
towns and countryside,
feeding hollow-eyed hundreds
who pursued him by day.
But a bottomless ocean
of hungry mouths
flooded his dreams.

He learned that the memory
of yesterday's bread
could not relieve today's hunger.

On the eve of his death
he at last found a way
to keep rejection and hunger
at bay. He held his life in his hands
and said to his friends,
"Take. Eat. This is my body,
broken for you."

And when they were filled, commanded:
"Feed the hungry. Do this.
Re-member me."

# And It Was Night

(John 13:30)

You stumble unseeing from the upper room
and no number of lanterns and torches can dim
your darkness now, Judas. When did you let
the light go out? When did you begin
to guard the hoard and spend starry evenings
behind drawn tent flaps, running the coins
through acquisitive fingers while the company sat
in a circle outside, breaking bread
and talking of light in the crackling campfire?

When did you fine-tune your ears to the clink
of copper and silver and gold, letting
the words of the Master fade out unheeded?
When did you start to begrudge begging hands
and when did you welcome disciples more
for the treasures they gave than the treasures they were?

Now, in the dark of Gethsemane's garden,
you touch greedy lips to the Master's cheek—
a cheap giveaway to your cohorts of night.

# As It Was in the Beginning

I spiral back
    toward the black
             mire
      from which You drew me,
                threw me
       on Your potter's wheel;
            feel
      Your hot
   nearness now,
Your fire;
      know not
         the how
           of death,
        know only that I must
    return this dust,
return to Breath.

# Crucifixion

Stripped of godliness,
hands hammered open,
arms yanked wide,
the crossbeamed Christ
pours himself out
till rivers run red with
wine enough to satisfy
century-cries of thirst.

# Pietà

The Sabbath hush
has stilled the rush
of the crucifying.
I'm numb with dying.
And could my tears
give more years
to my dead Son?

Yet even now
I know, somehow,
as they un-nail him
limb by limb
from the tree
and give him back to me,
that mothering goes on and on.

# V

# . . . And Rising

When darkness, stones, and tomb
bloomed to Easter morning,
she ran to him, shouting,
"This is my body, my blood!"

*(Liturgy)*

# Easter Song

*The wilderness and the dry land shall be glad,*
*the desert shall rejoice and blossom.*

*(Isaiah 35:1)*

Come to the garden with me!

Where we buried his humanity,
tombs have opened,
birds are singing.
Come and see!

Where we planted his humanity,
buds have opened,
flowers are blooming.
Come with me!

Come to the garden and see!

# Resurrection

Death, that
old snake
skin, lies
discarded at
the garden gate.

# The Women of Mark 16:8

"He is risen! He is not here!"
we heard—and fled
from the empty tomb,
our lips sealed by fear,
to cower in the upper room.

The Good News stayed dead
until, fed by the power
of Bread
broken,
we arose from our dread

and the Good News was spoken.

# Easter Witnesses

(Mark 16; Matthew 28)

The heady fragrances they carried
rose above their heads like incense,
exorcising the garden of death.
"Who will roll away the stone for us?"
the women whispered to one another.

Earlier, in the near-dawn darkness,
they had posed the question to the others—
as request, not challenge.
They had no heart to challenge the flock
hiding in terror behind secret doors.

None of the men had offered to go,
so the women had set out in haste alone
to straighten twisted feet and fingers,
comb black blood from matted hair,
anoint the precious body with spices.

"But who *will* roll away the stone?"
they whispered again as they neared the tomb.
"Jesus said prayer could move mountains.
We must stay together, continue to believe."
They stepped firmly forward, balancing their heavy jars.

When they looked up, they saw that the stone,
which was very large, had already been rolled back.
Inside, they heard from a being dressed in light:
"You are looking for Jesus who was crucified.
He has been raised; he is not here."

Fleeing from the tomb,
intent on telling no one,
they tripped pell-mell over terror and amazement
onto the glowing feet of Jesus.
"Go, tell the others!" he commanded.

After the telling, they set out in haste—
together this time, a community of equals—
to roll away stones, straighten crooked paths,
comb the far countries,
anoint the precious world with Good News.

# Emmaus Journey

(Luke 24:13–35)

All was chaos when he died.
We fled our separate ways at first,
then gathered again in the upper room
to chatter blue-lipped prayers
around the table where he'd talked
of love and oneness.

On the third day Cleopas and I
left for the home we'd abandoned
in order to follow him.
We wanted no part of the babble
the women had brought from the tomb.
We vowed to get on with our grieving.

On the road we met a Stranger
whose voice grew vaguely familiar
as he spoke of signs and suffering.
By the time we reached our village,
every tree and bush was blazing,
and we pressed him to stay the night.

Yet not till we sat at the table
and watched the bread being broken
did we see the light.

# Primacy

(John 20:3–8)

Though the other disciple won the race,
he waited at the tomb for Peter—
thus putting back in place the Rock
who, by his tumble out of grace,
had made himself a stumbling block.

# Liturgy

All the way to Elizabeth
and in the months afterward,
she wove him, pondering,
"This is my body, my blood!"

Beneath the watching eyes
of donkey, ox, and sheep,
she rocked him, crooning,
"This is my body, my blood!"

In the moonless desert flight
and the Egypt days of his growing,
she nourished him, singing,
"This is my body, my blood!"

In the search for her young lost boy
and the foreboding day of his leaving,
she let him go, knowing,
"This is my body, my blood!"

Under the blood-smeared cross,
she rocked his mangled bones,
re-membering him, moaning,
"This is my body, my blood!"

When darkness, stones, and tomb
bloomed to Easter morning,
she ran to him, shouting,
"This is my body, my blood!"

# VI
# Emmanuel: God with Us

finding every face
luminous
with godliness!
*(Emmanuel: God with Us)*

# Emmanuel: God with Us
(Galatians 3:26–28)

In Bethlehem
a baby's cry
shatters barriers.

Women, men
of every creed,
culture, race

gaze across
the rubbled walls
in wonder,

finding every face
luminous
with godliness!

# Theophany

What are we who tried so hard
    to keep you far from us,
    addressing you as God Most High,
    Lord, King, and offering gold on gold,
    clouds of incense, myrrh,
        to make of this?

What are we who tried so hard
    to save you from the smell
    of those below the bottom rung
    and now must step around still-steaming
    dung to reach your manger bed
        to make of this?

What are we who tried so hard
    to pick and purchase gifts of royal ilk
    and now see you, despite malodorous
    incense, drafty cold, move toward
    your mother's milk with infant bliss
        to make of this?

# A Woman's Journey
# in Discipleship

Jesus stood waiting for the woman's answer—
not looking past her, not laughing at her.
"Tell me what you need," he repeated, kindly,
"Come, what is it?"

"I don't need anything," she finally answered.
"I'm nothing but a . . ."
She didn't know how to finish the sentence.
She hung her head. "I'm nothing."

"Ah, you need a name," he said.
"I'll give you one: You-Are-Mine."

She thought he meant she was his slave,
so she followed the crowd that was following him.

After three days the people were hungry.
Jesus sat them down in small garden plots
and served fish and bread.
The woman ate with the rest.

When Jesus found her, he asked again,
"Do you know now what you need?"

"Please, Sir, I'm still hungry,"
she answered shyly.

He held out more bread.
"Take! Eat!" he told her.

"Let him put it down," she thought.
"I'm unclean."

It lay in his hands.
"Take it," Jesus urged.

She broke off a piece—
careful not to touch him—
and chewed it slowly, letting the mash
fill her mouth with its goodness.

He watched her swallow it
and asked, "Still hungry?"

She nodded.

"Take more."

When she reached for the bread,
her fingers touched his!
She backed away, frightened,
and awkwardly stumbled.

His right arm encircled her,
hemming her in.
"You-Are-Mine," he said,
"tell me what you need."

"If you please, Sir," she said,
"give me bread like this always."

"Those who follow me
never go hungry,"
he answered her, smiling.
"I am Living Bread."

# A Different Kind of King

On a night filled with stars,
Christ broke through our defenses,
disarming us with infant cries.
Kings from foreign countries
came to give him homage
but left again without a trace.

Years went by. Hearing nothing,
we regrouped, returned to battles.
He reappeared in the countryside,
recruiting the peasants
and sabotaging our strategies
by commands to love the enemy.

We infiltrated his company,
set him up as "King of the Jews,"
and nailed him for it on execution hill.
Now, rumors contend,
he has eastered back behind our lines
to plot a reign of peace.

# Pontius Pilate at the Therapist

You say it could as easily have been
Barabbas's blood the rabble asked for—
that it was their leaders who incited them.
But don't you see? That's it exactly, Sir!
The crowd called loud and clear for crucifixion.
One has to pay attention to a people
who obey like that. You did precisely
what you had to do. Now win their leaders'
loyalty and you've won the peace.
Sometimes a man, innocent or not,
has to die to pay the price of it.

The man was innocent, you say?
But don't forget you washed your hands of him—
a little water cleared you of the deed.
What a stroke of genius! Too bad
about your wife, though, washing her hands
a hundred times a day. No doubt in time
to come someone will make a play of it.
Tell her what's done is done—
what's one life less as long as it's not hers.
Perhaps you'd like to bring her, too, next time.

That's fifty denarii, please. Thank you, Sir.

# The Lost Parable

(Luke 15:1–10)

Luke placed the lost coin beside the lost sheep—
in parallel stories that show God's love
for every lost one of us.

Thus:
> *"What man among you*
> *having a hundred sheep*
> *and losing one of them . . .*
>> *"Or what woman*
>> *having ten coins*
>> *and losing one . . .*
> *"would not . . . go after the lost one*
> *until he finds it?*
>> *"would not . . . search carefully*
>> *until she finds it?*
> *"And when he does find it, . . .*
> *he calls together*
> *his friends and neighbors . . .*
>> *"And when she does find it,*
>> *she calls together*
>> *her friends and neighbors . . .*
> *"and says to them, 'Rejoice with me*
> *because I have found my lost sheep.'"*
>> *"and says to them, 'Rejoice with me*
>> *because I have found the coin that I lost.'"*

"In just the same way," Luke's Jesus concludes,
"his joy and hers are like the joy found in heaven
when a sinner returns."

Since the stories were written, hundreds of artists
have rescued lost lambs from their hazardous heights
by cradling them in the Good Shepherd's arms.

But the coin is still stuck in the cracks! Who will find it?

Who but a homemaker will sweep all the floors,
search drawers and shelves from attic to basement,
turn the house upside down, and never give up
till her broom uncovers the dust from the drachma!

When she has found it and calls us all in
to rejoice with her, may we see at last
whose image it bears—
*how the silver coin shines in the light of her eyes!*
*how it catches the glints of the silvery hair*
*of that Good Homemaker rejoicing in heaven!*

# Our Father Our Mother

Our Father Our Mother,
so wholly in heaven,
so on-the-way, so be-coming
in every him-her-you-me
that ever on earth
was, is, will-be,

knead us every this-day
into one bread.

# Easter

One thin slice of summer sandwiched between
childhood and adolescence, I traveled with
my mother and brothers through Nebraska.
Somewhere in the sand hills ten miles from
the nearest nowhere (the town's name forgotten now),
we found a river eastering out of the rocks,
all foam, all smiles, cavorting like wild colts
in twists and turns down the slope, carving out
a riverbed, and running into a rainbowed future.

My almost-adolescent self pulled off saddle shoes
and socks and stepped into that bright morning.

My mother and brothers, and the timid
woman-I-was-becoming tried to call her back,
but we lost sight of her as she and the river
swam downstream—lost sight until just now,
just this sudden morning when she burst through
the closed walls of the darkened room
where I'd fearfully gone to hide with my brothers
and stood dripping with sunlight, shouting,
"Jesus is alive! He said to meet him in Galilee."

This time, brothers, I refuse to stay behind.
Hurry, I already have my shoes off!

# Apple Picking: Eden Revisited

All day we played in paradise—
climbed up ladders into skies
of apple tree; shook, threw,
caught, ate the tempting fruit;
and laughed to see the legendary
serpent shrunk to harmless worms.

At evening, riding wagons home
with baskets crowned to overflowing,
we let go (without our knowing)
of the myth of up-and-downness—
saw God's graces in the roundness
of apples, baskets, earth, embraces.

# Feast of Saint Paul

This morning I had planned to pray
with Paul, knocked off his horse.

But oh! the birds, scarcely knowing what to do
with wings grown used to flying in a sodden sky
through days and days of rain on rain on rain,
circled, swooped, alit on bush and weed,
and filled the sun-rinsed air with fireworks
of melody that burst and bloomed and twinkled out
in slow descent into my prayer.

I tumbled into grace a different way
(whether in or out of the body, I don't know)
and saved Paul's route for a rainy day.

# A Celibate's Dialogue with God

I asked God:
    "Must I be my last and only word?
    Will this who-I-am be heard
    no more when I am dead?
    Who will know what I have said?
    Who will weave my melody into their song
    or hum at least my harmonies along
    with theirs? Who will? Who will?"

And God said: "Peace. Be still."

# On the Way to Easter

Bible in hand,
I slip behind a wall of time
to walk with the women.

"Are you afraid?" I ask,
panting to keep up with them—
strong from three years of walking.

"Of course," they answer,
"but his body must be anointed!"
They keep walking.

"There's no one to roll away
the stone," I object.
(Are they courageous or just naive?)

"There's no one else to anoint him,"
they counter, firmly,
and keep walking.

Ahead I see sunlight
glinting off steel. "There's no one
to protect you!" I protest.

They nod and keep walking,
their burdens perfectly balanced.
(Courageous, I decide.)

"Godspeed then," I say,
as I shift my life on my shoulders
and retreat to my safe, familiar world.

But the road on which I find myself
is crowded with people in need
of every kind of anointing.

"Godspeed!" I hear the women call
across the millennial wall
as I start walking.

# Dying and Rising

(for my brother)

In the silent tomb
of a Golgotha night
the sky opened
and I saw him
in a flash of forever,
drenched in starlight.

# Prayer for a Happy Death
(John 20:6–7)

When I arrive at the tomb,
petered out of breath like Peter,
let me enter it in awe,
see the worn garments of myself
neatly folded, laid aside,
and follow you anew in Galilee.

# Paschal Mystery

I am
growing,
eating the
white and yolk
inside this earth-
house; the shell is
beginning to harden a
bit, cramping me just
enough to let me know
this home is not for-
ever—someday I must
crack it open to
enter a larger
world.

## VII

# Return to Galilee

He must go back to where the Master
had found him. He must let Jesus find
him again.

*(Return to Galilee)*

# How the Mother of God Came to Be

Even before warning Adam and Eve not to eat of the Tree of Knowledge of Good and Evil, the Divine Persons called a meeting. The Creator posed the agenda to be discussed: What if the inconceivable happens and the couple chooses to eat of the Tree? They and their children will have to be redeemed.

"I was right there, playing in the world, when we made them in my image," said Wisdom. "If the worst scenario happens, I'll become one of them and show them how to live."

The Creator looked with Love at Wisdom. Love sighed, and said to Wisdom, "I'll go with you. I cannot be separated from you." With that the contingency plan was set in broad outline.

"Perhaps we should work out some of the details," said Wisdom. "Then if the couple does eat of the Tree, we can tell them about our plan right away so they won't die of despair."

"Any ideas?" asked the Creator.

"To begin with, how would I present myself to them? Would I just appear out of the blue one day and start talking to them?"

"You decide," said the other Two Persons. "It's you who would become the Human One."

"I'd rather it be a mutual decision," said Wisdom.

They breathed together for an eternal instant. Then Love broke out, "Would you be willing to begin from the beginning . . . as a baby? Everybody would love a baby!"

All Three smiled. It was a wonderful idea. Wisdom consented. But that solution led to another question, which they asked in the same breath: "What about a father and mother? A human baby has to have a father and mother."

The problem was enormous—how could they ask such small creatures to parent a human baby who was also divine? How could they create even one human person, much less two, who would be willing and able to take on such an unearthly responsibility?

"I could be an exception," said Wisdom. "I could have just one parent, and we could make it look as if I had both."

"Yes!" They breathed in unison.

"Which would you prefer, a mother or a father?" asked the Creator, ever the One to initiate.

"I'd like it to be our decision," Wisdom again replied.

Once more they were silent together for an eternal moment. Then all Three Persons smiled simultaneously.

"If they eat of the Tree," began Wisdom, looking almost eager for this to happen, "I'll have . . ."

Together they finished the sentence: "a mother!"

After the terrible ordeal of having to exile Adam and Eve from the garden, the Three set out in earnest to plan the details. Given the human culture in which Wisdom would have to accomplish the work of redemption, they decided to incarnate the Human One as a man.

"And I want to live very simply, so that no one will be afraid of me," Wisdom said. "I could be born as a refugee—maybe right out in a field or in a barn where the poor could easily come to visit me."

The Creator and Love readily agreed.

As centuries passed, they discussed the wonderful virtues of the mother. Finally, they talked about her physical gifts. "She'll need to be strong and healthy," said Love.

"She doesn't have to be the most exquisite woman we ever make," the Creator added, "but let's give her beautiful eyes."

"Yes," Love immediately concurred, "a mother's eyes are immensely important to a baby!"

The Trinity traveled Earth's past, present, and future history, searching for the right color. In twelfth-century France, they found a heavenly blue in the windows of the Cathedral of Notre Dame in Chartres. "Just perfect for a mother's eyes!" they exclaimed.

"But perhaps we should ask the human ones themselves what eye color they prefer in a mother," Wisdom suggested.

They called a council of artists. Each of them had a different opinion.

"Black!" shouted one.

"Brown!" shouted another with equal enthusiasm.

"Blue," murmured another artist, ecstatically.

"She should have a color so unique it hasn't been imagined yet," said a fourth.

"Yes, yes," they all agreed.

With that the Trinity quietly withdrew. "Dear artists," Wisdom smiled, "it will take them forever to imagine that color."

They continued the search until they found an ancient wise woman in the foothills of the Himalayas. "What color are the most beautiful eyes in the world?" they asked her.

"The color of my mother's eyes," she answered without hesitation.

The Trinity recognized her voice of authority. "And what color were her eyes?" they asked.

The old woman was silent for a long time.

"Well?" they asked, encouragingly.

"I don't remember," she finally replied. "To a baby, the most beautiful eyes in the world are those of its mother, no matter what the color."

That settled their inquiry. "We'll let it happen naturally," they decided.

When all was in readiness, the Trinity held a final meeting. From the beginning they had agreed that the woman they chose to be Mother of God must be totally free to accept or decline. Now they asked one another, "What if she says no? Should we prepare another contingency plan?"

Together they watched Mary of Nazareth finish watering the young fig trees in her parents' garden and move toward the house.

"She is so grace-filled," the Creator said, "such a highly favored daughter!"

Love nodded, murmuring, "Fair as the moon, bright as the sun!"

"I love her so much!" Wisdom said. "Let's just go ask her."

# The Refugees

Though the rocky outgrowth where she had hidden her tent provided shelter from the chill desert winds, the woman shivered as she stood in the entrance. Earlier in the night, she had felt safe. But now the rocks had consorted with the moon to create grotesque monsters around her. "They're only shadows," she reassured herself in a whisper. "They'll be gone in the morning."

A movement caught her eye as she turned to go back inside. Two people—one riding a donkey, the other on foot—were moving tiredly but steadily toward the shelter of her rocks. She waited, afraid.

"We'll stop here for a rest and begin again at sunup," she heard the one on foot say. "We've traveled far enough. We should be safe now."

"The Lord is protecting us," she heard a woman answer quietly.

The strangers saw the tent then—and saw her standing at its entrance watching them. They halted, motionless. A stray wind whistled between the boulders and caught the woman's veil. The bundle she held began to whimper.

"We mean no harm," the man finally broke the silence. "My name is Joseph. My wife, Mary, and I have been riding since darkness. Is your husband . . . ?"

She found his kind voice reassuring. "He's not here," she answered, "but you are welcome anyway. Your donkey will be safe behind the tent. And you'll find a bit of water there."

"Come, Mary, we'll be safe here," the man said. He reached up to help his wife dismount. She held the baby carefully.

The woman led Mary inside, toward the far corner where she had been sleeping. Mary drew the still-warm wrappings around the child and herself.

"Would you trust me to hold the baby while you rest?" the woman asked.

"You're so kind," Mary murmured. "If he begins to cry and is hungry . . ."

"Of course," the woman said, "I'll wake you." She took the baby and carefully sat on another pile of wrappings near the entrance. The child seemed to be asleep. She rocked him, holding him close.

Joseph came to the opening of the tent. "It's warm enough," he said quietly. "I'll stay out here to watch the donkey. Is my wife . . . ?"

"I think she's already asleep," the woman answered.

"Thank you for your kindness," Joseph said, and went back behind the tent.

The woman had nearly rocked herself to sleep when the baby began to stir in her arms. "Please don't be hungry," she whispered. She started to sing softly, her mouth close to the baby's ear: *"Ubi caritas et amor . . . ubi caritas, Deus ibi est."* The baby grew still. She hummed the song over and over.

The stars were beginning to dim when Mary spoke quietly into the darkness, "You are very good with the child. He didn't cry at all during the night." She came over and sat beside the woman.

"I watched you and your husband coming up the wadi," the woman confided. "At first I was so afraid. There was no place to hide."

"Terrible things can happen to a woman alone in the dark," Mary answered. "Is your husband away for long?"

"I have no husband," the woman answered. "I was led to the desert—to face my demons. Or so I had thought. Then you came." Suddenly she was crying.

Mary gently touched her arm, but said nothing, waiting.

"I've been afraid all my life," the woman finally continued. "I'm so ashamed."

The child woke up and demanded to be fed this time. They listened to him suckling.

"I know what it is to be afraid," Mary said.

"You?" the woman questioned.

"We were warned very strangely. Joseph had a terrible dream. He woke me up and said someone wanted to kill our baby and we must be far away by daylight. We only had time to gather what food and water we had on hand. Somehow we found our way out of the city in the dark. I tried to stay calm so the child would not be frightened and cry. Babies can feel when one is afraid, you know."

"Yes," the woman agreed.

Silence rested comfortably between them.

The woman spoke again, with wonder in her voice, "You were fleeing for your baby's life, and yet you trusted me to watch him while you slept?"

"I needed rest," Mary said. "You offered it. I felt the Lord had sent you."

The woman felt tears coming again. "Could I travel with you, back to my people?" she asked at last.

"Of course," Mary answered. "We could take turns carrying the child. That would be of great help."

The dusty sky ahead told the three of them that they were nearing the city. "It's your turn to rest, Joseph," Mary said.

He nodded and helped her down. The women had insisted, until he reluctantly agreed, that he ride part of the way. He had to keep up his strength, they said, for whatever the day would bring. An elder of the synagogue had once mentioned that there were still kinfolk in Egypt. But how would they find them?

The two women walked side by side in silence. When Mary saw Joseph's head nodding, she said quietly, "Your people are not from this land." It was a statement rather than a question, but she had no accusation in her voice.

"How did you come to know?" the woman asked.

"While you were riding, the wind caught your cloak, and I saw clothing I did not recognize."

"I'm from the United States," the woman said. "We call them jeans."

When they reached the outskirts of the city, Joseph awoke.

"Thank you for letting me travel with you," the woman said to him. "You and Mary will find your own people now, and I must go home to mine."

The two women embraced in the dusty road, holding the child between them.

"The baby slept well in your arms," Mary said. "He trusts you."

"All generations love you and call you blessed," the woman said.

# Firstborn Son

Already lamps were being lit in the houses in the valley. From the other side of the table, Jesus studied his mother's face in the gathering dusk. The shock of her disclosure had made him speechless—Joseph had not begotten him!

"He was such a gentle man," Mary finally continued. "He could have had me stoned, you know. Or publicly denounced and put away."

They were in the kitchen. The burial was over and the last of the villagers had gone home. "Joseph the Just One," people had named him over and over as they told their stories. . . .

Miriam had come, shepherding her five-year-olds. "When we ordered a cradle, we didn't expect twins," she had said, gratefully. "Joseph built and delivered a second cradle on the very day these two were born. He said since Yahweh had given two for the price of one, he would do the same."

"We used our table and chairs for thirteen years before we could pay for them," Simon their neighbor had said. "Joseph always told us, 'Money can wait. Meals can't.'"

"Joseph made wood come alive when he touched it," the widow Naomi had told them. "The chest he built for Jacob and me is as beautiful now as it was on our wedding day."

"Joseph and I had planned to tell you after your bar mitzvah," Mary continued, "but when we lost you in Jerusalem and then finally found you in the Temple, you seemed so distant. And when you said we should have known you would be in your Father's house, I thought it had been revealed to you somehow."

Her words brought back the strange feelings he had experienced that day, and he could finally speak again. "When the Doctors were explaining the prophecies of Isaiah, I had such a longing to hold the scroll in my hands. I felt as if my life were written there, waiting for me to unroll it."

They sat in silence, sharing their pain at last.

"We can only listen and wait until we know how to obey," Mary said.

"I listen and listen, wait and wait," Jesus confided. "I start a day's work of making tables and chairs. I get completely engrossed in them. Then, even before they're finished, they stand there looking at me as if they know something about my future. I come home for supper and even the plates and cups seem to hold secrets about me."

"Yes, I see that too," she said.

He brought his hand to her cheek and felt her tears.

"When your time comes to leave, I will go to my sister," she said, quietly. "You were born for other reasons than to take care of a widowed mother."

He understood that she had already foreseen his problem and found a way to release him from his duties as firstborn son.

"I feel the time is coming soon—that I must be ready," he confided.

"Yes, my son, I know," she nodded in the evening darkness.

# Peter's Call to Discipleship

(Luke 5:1–11; Luke 12:22–32)

We docked our boat close to where the Master was talking and started to clean our nets. I guess Andrew felt as tired as I did, after spending the whole night out there without catching a thing. We didn't pay much attention to him at first. But he had a kind voice, and what he was saying helped me get my thoughts off the awful night we'd had, even though he sounded pretty idealistic.

The usual crowd of cripples, beggars, women, kids, and old folks were around him. He must have just finished a story. If there was anything people liked about him, it was his storytelling. You know you've got a good storyteller when the kids keep still. I never in my life saw so many kids keep still together.

I was untangling the last of the seaweed from our net when I heard him say, "Therefore I tell you, do not worry about your life, what you will eat, or about your body, what you will wear. For life is more than food, and the body more than clothing." I got rid of the seaweed, but it was harder to shake his words loose. "That's easy enough to say," I thought, "but he should try telling my wife that."

Just about then he stopped talking and looked toward us. When I saw how tired he was and how the crowd was pushing and shoving, I motioned to our boat. He nodded and came over.

Andrew and I towed him away from the shore a bit and jumped aboard. I was planning to take him out into the lake so he could rest—maybe get a little sleep. But the Master looked at the birds flying around our boat and started talking to the crowd again.

"Consider the ravens: they neither sow nor reap, they have neither storehouse nor barn, and yet God feeds them," he said. "Of how much more value are you than the birds!"

Some of that made sense, I thought. Even with her worst headache, my mother-in-law would probably agree I was worth more than her pigeons. But it had been a while since the skies rained down manna. I wasn't exactly ready to believe that the Lord was about to put fish on my table without a lot of help from me.

Jesus was still talking. "Do not keep striving for what you are to eat and what you are to drink, and do not keep worrying. . . . Instead, strive for your Father's kingdom, and these things will be given to you as well."

He looked straight at me then. I thought he'd wound up his talk and wanted us to take him farther out. But he added, looking toward the shore again, "Do not be afraid, little flock, for it is your Father's good pleasure to give you the kingdom."

Everybody just stood there, perfectly still. I tell you, he had a power about him. The way he talked about God as his Father made you think God really cared if you lived or died—maybe even cared if you didn't catch any fish. So when the Master turned back to me and said, "Put out into the deep water, and let down your nets for a catch," I told him, "Master, we have worked all night long but have caught nothing. Yet if you say so, I will let down the nets."

Well, as soon as our nets hit the water, there was a ruckus you wouldn't believe. I never saw so many fish! They were actually jumping out of the water, trying to get to the nets. Luckily for us, John and James were coming in just then. We called them over to help us before our nets broke.

Even after we'd thrown the smaller fish back, both our boats were full. I looked at all those fish and thought about what the Master had told us—that God really cares if people go hungry or have nothing to put on. All at once I got scared. Who was this man, calling God "Father" and pulling off a miracle like that? I got down on my knees right there in the middle of all those fish—I didn't care what Andrew or James or John thought—and begged him, "Go away from me, Lord, for I am a sinful man!"

And then something happened that for me was an even bigger miracle. Jesus took my hand and looked at me without saying a word. He didn't have to—I knew exactly what he was thinking. "You're a sinful man, all right, Simon," he was telling me. "You talk too much, too quickly, and too loud. But when you talk, people pay attention. If you tell them to listen to me, they'll say, 'Simon wouldn't lose his head over some wild-eyed preacher who's really a tax collector in disguise.' You aren't perfect, but I can use you. Will you follow me?"

When Jesus finally dropped my hand, I felt changed. Oh, I knew I could still clean nets and handle a boat. But he was offering me his own power and goodness. And I could either use them to touch other people, even to make those cripples on shore able to walk home on their own two feet if he wanted me to, or I could refuse him. But if I said no to him, I'd be my same old self for the rest of my life.

He said aloud then, talking to the four of us, "Do not be afraid; from now on you will be catching people."

We took the boats in and left them there, with all those fish still wiggling in them. We could do nothing else. He had asked us to follow him.

# The Healing
(Luke 8:43–48)

The woman poured the last of the water on the stone floor and carefully wiped up the flour she had spilled while making bread. She would have to go for more water to clean the outside steps. But she didn't mind. The morning was still cool, and she felt better now—the scrubbing had relieved her cramps.

She walked rapidly toward the well for the third time that morning, thinking of what her sister Miriam had said last evening when she'd brought the flour: "People call you 'unclean,' and yet you are the cleanest woman in Galilee. Why do you work so hard? Do you think Ezra will show up again at your doorstep? He won't, you know."

Of course, she knew. She no longer felt any bitterness toward her former husband. He wasn't to blame for her constant flow of blood. It was Jairus, the leader of the synagogue, who had urged the divorce. "It's a man's duty to raise sons," he had said, "and two years is a long enough time for a woman to give you one."

Ezra had been generous enough. If she hadn't spent it all on doctors these past ten years, she'd probably still have money enough to buy her own flour. "Well," she shrugged, "let Miriam scold me for all the scrubbing. I have to do what I can to get rid of my uncleanness."

She had almost reached the well when she saw the women. Strangers in town! Their presence could mean only one thing—Jesus, the wonder-worker, had come. Instantly she turned down an alley, nearly dropping the largest of her water jars as she ran back home.

The freshly washed floor felt cool to her bare feet. Sitting on the stone bench, she leaned against the clean adobe wall. "What a fool I am," she told herself, feeling her resolve begin to seep away like a slow leak in a cracked jar. "How can I dare even to go near him, much less to touch him? And why would he want to cure me?" Taunting, boyish shouts of "Unclean! Unclean!" flooded her memory. She shuddered.

Then she jumped to her feet, flung off her apron, grabbed an inconspicuously dark shawl, and ran out without waiting for the door to slam behind her. Halfway down the alley, she heard the door creak open again, and she remembered the broken latch. But she couldn't trust herself to go back. "Let thieves break in if they want to," she thought. "They won't find much."

Two Sabbaths had passed since she'd given her last coins to the new doctor in payment for the cure he had not given her. "It's not my fault you're such a hopeless case," he had said, disdainfully. "It's clear that you or your parents were greater sinners than any of my other patients."

At the street corner, she saw people running toward the synagogue. "That must be where the wonder-worker is," she thought. She dashed down a side alley, taking familiar shortcuts until she arrived at the building. She pulled her outer garments closely around her and waded into the crowd.

When she caught sight of the approaching Master, she stopped short. "I can't touch him—a rabbi!" she thought. But then she remembered the stories Miriam had heard at the well. He seemed to have no fear of ritual uncleanness. He had touched and cured lepers, paralytics, the blind, the deaf—even a demoniac! Last week, while he was dining in the house of Simon the Pharisee, a prostitute had burst into the room, bathed his feet with her tears, and wiped them with her hair. Afterward, instead of scolding her, he had publicly praised her. In the town of Nain a fortnight ago, he had even touched a corpse!

Resolutely, she pushed her fears away. "I'll just touch the tip of his tassel," she told herself. "The Master won't feel it, and in this crowd no one will notice." She smiled beneath her veil as she remembered that tassels were intended to remind their wearers to keep the Law.

Just then she recognized the man walking next to Jesus. Jairus, of all people! How carefully he had instructed her of her responsibility to avoid touching men. "He must not see me!" she thought. Quick as the blink of a hen's eye, her hand darted out and touched the tassel. She swam back into the crowd.

The sun broke through clouds inside her, flooding her with clear blue sky. Flowers blossomed. Field lilies poured out their fragrance.

Chickadees chirped. A lark called her by name. Finally, she realized the lark's voice was not inside her but outside, asking with an urgency that had no anger in it, "Who touched me?"

She heard a robust man with a pool of black curls washing over his forehead say, "But, Master, in this crowd? How can you ask? Everybody is touching you. Nobody is touching you!"

She heard the rabbi insisting, "Someone touched me. I felt power go out from me." In an instant she understood: he wanted to *know* the people he healed! He didn't want to be used like magic. Overcoming her fear, she stepped forward, flung herself at his feet, and confessed, "Master, it was I who touched you. You have cured me!"

"Daughter," he said, resting his hand on her shawled head. "Your faith has made you well; go in peace."

The words washed over her like cleansing rain. She stood up and followed him down the street toward Jairus's house.

# Return to Galilee

It was already the ninth hour when Peter arrived in Capernaum. He stopped for a drink at the village well; then he walked to the house of Jacob and Esther, whose wedding the newly formed company had attended. How good the wine had tasted that day! How proud he had been to be recognized as a disciple of Jesus, the wonder-worker.

At his knock, Esther, big with child, came to the door. A toddler peeked out from behind her skirts, shyly returned his smile, and disappeared again. "Have you seen Jesus?" Peter asked the woman. He hoped she wouldn't press him for news.

"But weren't you with him yourself in Jerusalem?" she exclaimed in surprise. "We heard he was crucified!"

So Capernaum already knew. "It's true. On the eve of the Sabbath. He hung on the cross for three hours before he died." His voice began to break, and his mouth clamped shut. He nodded an abrupt good-bye and quickly walked away.

He searched every street and alley, and finally headed out of town. Though the footpath was not well marked and sometimes disappeared altogether, he picked his way quite easily up the hill overlooking the Sea of Galilee. During the early months, he had often watched Jesus head toward the rock ledge at the top. Once he had searched and found the Master there, absorbed in prayer, looking out over the valley.

Yes, that was where Jesus would be waiting—if the two Marys' story could be believed. Perhaps the awful shock of the Crucifixion had been too much for them. Peter thought again of the women as they breathlessly repeated the message that they said an angel had given them: "He has been raised from the dead, and indeed he is going ahead of you to Galilee; there you will see him."

What if the story were true? What would he say to Jesus? What could he say? Tears stung his eyes—impossible now to understand how he had come to deny the Master so vehemently. Would he be forever bobbing up and down, walking on and sinking in the water, relying one moment on Jesus and the next moment on himself?

Peter's breath came in gasps as he reached the rock ledge. He halted, torn for a moment between dread and anticipation. Then the dread was gone, and he was filled with an overwhelming longing to see Jesus, to beg his forgiveness, to know again the joy and peace he had always felt in his presence. He ran along the path that led behind the rocks, calling the Master's name.

No one was sitting on the rocks, waiting. Even the birds had flown away. Peter sank heavily onto a stony ledge and cried in bitter aloneness.

In his dream he was out fishing. Suddenly, he saw Jesus standing on the water a short distance from the boat, saying, "Peter, Peter, didn't I tell you that you would deny me? Didn't I tell you that I would pray for you?" Afterward, Jesus was standing on the shore, calling, "Have you caught anything?" Peter shook his head, unable to say a word. "Then you know what you must do."

When he woke, the sun was already hanging low in the sky behind him. He sat stone-still, staring at the empty rocks facing him, then at the lake below. Its flat surface reflected his own lifelessness back to him. Suddenly, the sun's last rays turned the lake into a blaze of light, beckoning him. He forced himself to his feet, and took the path leading down to the shore.

Except for the gulls, he was alone on the beach. A short distance away, one of them stood motionless, eyeing the water. A wave came in, moved up its spindly legs, retreated again down the sandy beach. A second wave rolled in and crept up toward it. The bird took off, flying far out across the water, searching the empty sea, crying. It circled back toward shore, then out again, over and over, calling him.

"I'm going fishing," Peter said aloud, and walked decisively toward the boats. He must start over. He must go back to where the Master had found him. He must let Jesus find him again.

# The Homemaker God

(Luke 15:8–10)

The Homemaker God has come to my house
to search for the lost coin of me
which I, in my miserly morning,
thinking this frugal and wise
and worthy of praise and grace,
hid in a safe "good place."

The Homemaker God has taken her broom
and swept from attic to basement,
moved cupboards and dressers,
stripped beds, emptied drawers—
now she's checking each pantry shelf
for the silver coin of myself.

The Homemaker God will find me, I trust—
she knows how to raise dust.

**Acknowledgments** *(continued)*

The scriptural quotation in "The Lost Parable" is from the New American Bible with revised Psalms and revised New Testament. Copyright © 1991, 1986, and 1970 by the Confraternity of Christian Doctrine, 3211 Fourth Street NE, Washington, DC 20017. All rights reserved.

All other scriptural quotations are from the New Revised Standard Version of the Bible. Copyright © 1989 by the Division of Christian Education of the National Council of the Churches of Christ in the United States of America. All rights reserved.

Some of these poems have appeared previously, as follows:

*The Christian Century:* "And It Was Night"; "Apple Picking: Eden Revisited"; "Resurrection"; "Woman Un-Bent"

*Emmanuel:* "Cana Wine"; "'How Can This Be, Since I Am a Virgin?'"; "The Lost Parable"; "A Woman's Journey in Discipleship"

*Newman of Oxford* (Wyndham Hall Press): "As It Was in the Beginning"

*WomenPsalms* (Julia Ahlers et al., eds., Saint Mary's Press) and *Catholic Women's Network:* "Liturgy"

*Review for Religious:* "Pietà"

*Sisters Today:* "Incarnation"

*St. Anthony Messenger:* "Blind Trust"; "First Forgiveness"; "First Word"; "The Homemaker God"; "Litany for Ordinary Time"; "Paschal Mystery"

## About the Author

Irene Zimmerman, a School Sister of Saint Francis, grew up among many siblings on a farm near Westphalia, Iowa. As a child she learned to love music and the arts, and discovered early that poetry was a way of making music and painting pictures with words. She began writing poetry intermittently—as a child during summer vacations when the school library was closed, and later as she taught high school English and French in Milwaukee.

Irene's "official" ministry has taken her from Milwaukee to Germany and back to Milwaukee. She has worked in a boarding school, in various clerical positions, and most recently as part of the academic support staff at Alverno College; but she has come to regard poetry writing as a significant part of her prayer and ministry. Writing poetry brings her to a sense of awe at the wonders of creation and for the Creator who "so loves the world."